THE WHIPPING BOY

The Whipping Boy

by
SID FLEISCHMAN

illustrations by PETER SIS

Troll Associates

A TROLL BOOK, published by Troll Associates

Published by arrangement with Greenwillow Books, a division of
William Morrow & Company, Inc. For information address
Greenwillow Books, William Morrow & Company, Inc., 105
Madison Avenue, New York, New York 10016.

First Troll Printing, 1987

Printed in the United States of America

20   19   18   17

ISBN 0-8167-1038-4

*For
David Avadon*

CHAPTER 1
In which we observe a hair-raising event

The young prince was known here and there (and just about everywhere else) as Prince Brat. Not even black cats would cross his path.

One night the king was holding a grand feast. Sneaking around behind the lords and ladies, Prince Brat tied their powdered wigs to the backs of their oak chairs.

Then he hid behind a footman to wait.

When the guests stood up to toast the king, their wigs came flying off.

The lords clasped their bare heads as if they'd been scalped. The ladies shrieked.

Prince Brat (he was never called that to his face, of course) tried to keep from laughing. He clapped both hands over his mouth. But out it ripped, a cackle of *hah-hah*s and *haw-haw*s and *hee-hee-hees*.

The king spied him and he looked mad enough to spit ink. He gave a furious shout.

"Fetch the whipping boy!"

Prince Brat knew that he had nothing to fear. He had never been spanked in his life. He was a prince! And it was forbidden to spank, thrash, cuff, smack, or whip a prince.

A common boy was kept in the castle to be punished in his place.

"Fetch the whipping boy!"

The king's command traveled like an echo from guard to guard up the stone stairway to a small chamber in the drafty north tower.

An orphan boy named Jemmy, the son of a rat-catcher, roused from his sleep. He'd been dreaming happily of his ragged but carefree life before he'd been plucked from the streets and sewers of the city to serve as royal whipping boy.

A guard shook him fully awake. "On your feet, me boy."

Jemmy's eyes blazed up. "Ain't I already been whipped twice today? Gaw! What's the prince done now?"

"Let's not keep the great folks waitin', lad."

In the main hall, the king said, "Twenty whacks!"

Defiantly biting back every yelp and cry, the whipping boy received the twenty whacks. Then

the king turned to the prince. "And let that be a lesson to you!"

"Yes, Papa." The prince lowered his head so as to appear humbled and contrite. But all the while he was feeling a growing exasperation with his whipping boy.

In the tower chamber, the prince fixed him with a scowl. "You're the worst whipping boy I ever had! How come you never bawl?"

"Dunno," said Jemmy with a shrug.

"A whipping boy is supposed to yowl like a stuck pig! We dress you up fancy and feed you royal, don't we? It's no fun if you don't bawl!"

Jemmy shrugged again. He was determined never to spring a tear for the prince to gloat over.

"Yelp and bellow next time. Hear? Or I'll tell Papa to give you back your rags and kick you back into the streets."

Jemmy's spirits soared. Much obliged, Your Royal Awfulness! he thought. I'll take me rags, and I'll be gone in the half-blink of an eye.

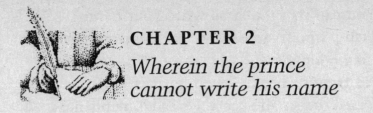

CHAPTER 2

*Wherein the prince
cannot write his name*

Jemmy could count on a thrashing first thing in the morning. Sure and certain, he thought, as he pulled on his fine velvet breeches and silk stockings. The prince wouldn't know his lessons, the royal tutor was quick as a flyswatter with his willow switch—and Jemmy would be back in rags.

"Take a last look at me, Pa, rest your bones," he muttered to himself. "Did you ever think I'd be holed up in the king's own castle and all rigged up in duds would shame a peacock? Reckon I'll fetch a pair of sharp-toothed ferrets and go to rat-catchin', same as you. Same as you, Pa."

The tutor, Master Peckwit, was a round-faced man with fat cheeks. He pointed his switch at the prince.

"You fiddle-faddled scholar!" he bellowed. "One day you'll be king! And you still don't know the alphabet from pig tracks!"

The prince snapped his fingers. "I can always get someone to read for me."

"You can't so much as write your name!"

"Pish-posh. I can always get someone to write my name for me."

The tutor's cheeks, swelling with anger, almost unhorsed the small spectacles saddling his nose. "It would be easier to educate a boiled cabbage! Prepare to be punished, Your Lordship!"

"Ten whacks at least," said the prince. "And good and hard, if you please."

Jemmy, who was obliged to be close at hand for the daily lessons, reckoned that freedom was now close at hand. The prince threw him a smirking glance as Master Peckwit raised the switch and beat the whipping boy like a carpet.

Jemmy didn't bawl. He didn't yelp or bellow. Ten whacks, and not a sound escaped his lips.

"You contrary rascal!" the prince exploded. "I'm on to you, Jemmy-From-The-Streets. It's pure spite that you won't howl! Think you can cross me and get away with it? Ha! Never and nohow!"

Gaw! thought Jemmy. He's going back on his word!

"And don't try to run away. I'll have you tracked down till your tongue hangs out like a red flag!"

And so it went for more than a year. The prince learned nothing. The whipping boy learned to read, write, and do sums.

CHAPTER 3
The runaways

On a night when the moon gazed down like an evil eye, the young prince appeared in Jemmy's chamber.

"Boy! Tumble out of bed. I need a manservant."

Jemmy saw that the prince was wearing a black cloak and carrying a wicker basket the size of a sea chest. "What you up to now? Walkin' in your royal sleep, are you?"

"I'm running away."

The whipping boy sat bolt upright. Hardly a day passed that he didn't make one plan or another to run off—but a prince? What horrible new mischief was this? "You can't hop off like you was common folks. What's bitin' you?"

Said the prince, "I'm bored."

"With dumping bullfrogs in the moat so no one got a wink o' sleep?"

"Boring."

"And didn't you laugh fit to kill when the knights slipped off their horses and clattered to the ground? You'd hog-greased the saddles."

The prince folded his arms. "Boring."

"And don't you get me thrashed so that this hide o' mine feels like the devil run me over with spikes in his shoes?"

"Let's be off!"

Why me? Jemmy thought. Can't you find a friend to run off with? But no—not you, Prince Brat. You've got no friends. That's why me.

Jemmy pointed to the window. "It's night out," he protested.

"The best time," replied the prince.

"But ain't you afraid o' the dark? Everyone knows that! You won't even sleep without a lit candle."

"Lies! Anyway, the moon's up, good and bright. Come on."

Jemmy stared at him with dreadful astonishment. "The king'll have a gory-eyed fit!"

"Positively."

"He'll hunt us down. You'll get off light as a feather, but I'll be lucky if they don't whip me to the bone. More likely I'll be hung from the gallows. Scragged for sure!"

"Your lookout," said the prince with a dry grin. "Carry the basket, Jemmy-From-The-Streets, and follow me!"

CHAPTER 4
Containing hands in the fog

The night moon had lit their way like a lantern.

But by dawn the runaways, double-mounted on a horse from the castle stable, were hopelessly lost. A thick fog had swirled in, they'd strayed from the road, and trees had closed in on them.

"Forests is creepy things," said Jemmy, hanging on to the basket as best he could. "Gimme cobbled streets anytime."

A low branch almost swept them off the saddle.

"Boy," said the prince, "get down and lead this dumb-headed beast."

"Lead it? In this fog? I'd need two hands and a lantern to find me own nose."

But Jemmy slipped off the saddle. A plan had been tumbling about in his head. Here's your chance, Jemmy, he told himself. Slip away in the fog. Run for it! No more whippings for you, not if you can't be found. The great sewers, Jemmy, that's the place to hide!

"What's keeping you?" asked the prince. "Grab the halter."

"I'm thinkin'."

Leaves crackled under Jemmy's feet as he began to back off. His mind was made up. Once the fog cleared, he'd find the river. Hadn't his pa taught him his way through the maze of mighty brick sewers! That's where they'd caught the fiercest rats to sell by the cageful. The dog-and-rat pits paid fancy prices for the best fighters, and that meant sewer rats. Who'd think to look for Jemmy under the city?

Jemmy took another crackling step backward— and froze. A sudden yellow glow floated in the fog. The prince burst into squawks and bellows.

"Who's there? Let go! Take your hands off me, you insolent rascal!"

There came a rough, booming reply. "Well, what we got here?" The glowing lantern swayed. "A noisy brat on a fine beast of a horse."

Jemmy edged closer. A cutthroat! he thought.

Like a snake striking, a ghostly hand darted through the fog and clutched his arm. A second cutthroat! Jemmy looked up and barely made out a long, bony face with hollow cheeks and a nose like a meat cleaver.

"I got another, Billy!" cackled the second man, shoving Jemmy forward.

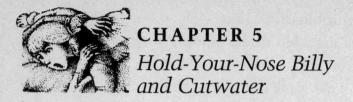

CHAPTER 5
Hold-Your-Nose Billy and Cutwater

Billy pulled Prince Brat from the saddle and threw him into Jemmy.

Raising the lantern, the man held it close enough that Jemmy could feel the heat of the flame. Billy was a big man, he saw, big and raw as a skinned ox. And he smelled like a ton of garlic.

"Not much of a catch—two sparrows," said Billy. "But ain't they trimmed up in fancy rags, Cutwater?"

"Ain't they!" echoed the rattleboned man.

"Got any gold in your pockets, lads?"

"No business of yours!" snapped the prince.

"Ah, but so help me, it *is* my business," Billy said with a thunderclap of laughter. "Don't you know who I am?"

"A clod and a ruffian," declared the prince.

"Worse'n that!" corrected the big man. "Ain't you never heard of Hold-Your-Nose Billy?"

"Famous, he is," put in Cutwater. "Put to song, is Billy."

Jemmy thought he remembered. Hadn't he heard ballad sellers fling that name about the streets? The exploits of Hold-Your-Nose Something-or-other in verses by the yard? "The highwayman, are you?"

"The same."

"The murderer?"

"Only in the line of duty," Hold-Your-Nose Billy chuckled. "So you won't mind if we take your horse and empty your pockets."

"Not a copper between us," said Jemmy. A prince didn't carry money, for he had no use for it, and Jemmy's accounts were kept on the books.

"What's in the basket?" piped up Cutwater.

"Hands off, villain!" snapped Prince Brat. "Don't you know who *I* am?"

Jemmy gave the prince a sudden jab of his elbow to keep his mouth shut. Not a word!

But the heir to the throne raised himself to his full height. "Bow to your prince!"

Fog swirled around the lantern. "Bow to what?" asked Cutwater.

"I am Prince Horace!"

"And I'm the Grand Turnip of China!" Cutwater snickered.

"Dim-witted villains!" shouted the prince. "I command you to turn us loose. Or Papa will hang the pair of you in chains!"

Hold your trap! Jemmy thought. Don't you have a thimbleful of brains? A prince would make a fine catch for these rogues. "Me friend's muddle-headed," he declared. "His paw's nothing but a rat-catcher. But don't he put on airs, though!"

"Got enough lip for two sets of teeth," chortled the big highwayman. "Cutwater, take the lantern and fetch the horse."

"What do you reckon's in the basket, Billy?"

"Plenty of time to find out."

The lantern floated off. The evil-smelling Billy clutched each boy hard by the ear.

"Stir your legs. Walk! And don't let me catch you on our turf again. Do I make myself clear?"

"Clear as window glass," said Jemmy with a sigh of relief. "If you'd be kind enough to point us toward the river, I'd be ever so much obliged."

"Billy!" came a shout from Cutwater. "They ain't just common sparrows. Have a look at this saddle."

Hold-Your-Nose Billy hung on to the boys' ears. At the horse's side, Cutwater was holding the lantern close to the saddle.

"Skin me alive!" declared the big man in awe. "That's the king's own crest."

14

"We stole it, horse and saddle!" Jemmy put in desperately.

"Bosh!" retorted Prince Brat scornfully. "Didn't I tell you who I was? Bow low, you fools, and be off!"

But the two men neither bowed nor fled. Hold-Your-Nose Billy threw a bushy-eyed glance at his fellow outlaw.

"Cutwater, what do you reckon a genuine prince on the hoof is worth?"

"His weight in gold at least, Billy."

CHAPTER 6
In which the plot thickens

Wisps of fog clung like tattered rags to the trees, and then the forest cleared. But so thick were the pines that the morning sun barely touched the ground.

Hold-Your-Nose Billy pushed aside a low branch, revealing a rickety timbered hut with a moldy thatched roof.

"There's our castle, Your Young Majesty," he said, chuckling. "Accept our hospitality! I hope you won't mind sleeping on the floor."

The floor was hard-packed earth. Braided garlic bulbs hung like knotted ropes from the rafters.

"I'm hungry," announced Prince Brat.

"And feast you will," said Hold-Your-Nose Billy. "Cutwater, serve 'em up our finest bread and herring."

Jemmy had made many a meal on bread and herring, when he was in luck, and felt hungry enough to ask for seconds.

Prince Brat bared his teeth. "I'd sooner eat mud!" He reached for the wicker basket, but Cutwater snatched it back.

"What we got here?" muttered the bone-thin man, and threw back the lid. "Roll your eyes at this, Billy! Meat pies, looks like, and fruit tarts— and a brace of roast pheasant! We'll eat like kings!"

"Hands off—that's mine!" the prince cried out.

"*Was* yours," yapped Cutwater.

Lawks! Jemmy thought. Hadn't the prince run away in royal style! He had even brought a China plate, a silver spoon, and a silver knife for himself.

Digging around deeper in the basket, the garlicky outlaw called out to Cutwater. "Bring the lantern closer! What's this?"

In the gloom of the hut, the big man lifted out a golden crown.

"That's mine!" bleated the prince.

"*Was* yours," corrected Hold-Your-Nose Billy, placing the crown on the tangled red nest of his hair.

"Prince Hold-Your-Nose Billy!" Cutwater burst out joyously. He began to scratch himself as if his shirt were crawling with fleas, which, Jemmy thought, it probably was. "We're dog rich!"

"That crown? A trifle," scoffed Hold-Your-Nose Billy. "We can be richer 'n dog rich."

The empty-headed prince! Jemmy thought. Why had he brought along his crown? To cock it on his head and expect vagabonds and cutthroats to fall to their knees?

The big, raw-faced outlaw grabbed Prince Brat off the ground and took the heft of him as if he were weighing a sack of potatoes.

"Fifty-five pounds, by my reckoning," he said. "We'll write the king a command, Cutwater. Fifty-five pounds of gold coin in trade for his royal tadpole."

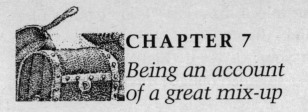

CHAPTER 7
*Being an account
of a great mix-up*

Cutwater rummaged around in a black oak chest of stolen goods. Handkerchiefs flew out like soiled white doves, worn shoes, ladies' combs, a cowbell—a junk heap. They've had lean pickings, this raggedy pair of highwaymen, Jemmy thought. And maybe not as smart and clever as the song sellers made out.

"Here's a scrap of paper, Billy," said Cutwater, finding it in the pocket of a stolen coat. "But how are we going to do the scribblement? We can't write."

"I've seen it done. Sharpen us a hawk's feather, Cutwater."

"I'm *hungry*," complained the prince. "I'll have a veal pie, sir!"

Hold-Your-Nose Billy ignored him. He poked around for a beet root and squeezed out the juice with his bare hand. It dripped like blood onto a China plate. "There's ink for you, Prince. Take the hawk's feather and scratch out our message."

Prince Brat folded his arms. "I don't take orders from curs and villains."

"Think of your pa," said Hold-Your-Nose Billy. "He'll be ever so much obliged to know you're safe and hearty."

"I told you I'm hungry!"

"You won't eat a bean till you do us the document."

"But I can't write!" blurted out Prince Brat.

"And crows can't fly!" erupted the big outlaw with a blast of garlicky breath. "You're a prince! Kings and such-like are learned to write and read soon as they tumble out of the cradle. Don't think you can pull the wool over our eyes. Hop to it!"

"But I can't so much as scratch my own name!"

Jemmy shot a calculating glance at Prince Brat. His pesky hide hardly seemed worth saving, but a scheme had leaped into his head. He might be able to trick these mangy outlaws into letting the prince go. And Jemmy would be rid of Prince Brat once and for all.

"Give *me* the hawk's quill. I'll write the words," he announced.

"That's right," Prince Brat chimed in. "My whipping boy knows his letters. Fall to, Jemmy-From-The-Streets."

"Hold on," said Hold-Your-Nose Billy, his sharp gaze flicking from one boy to the other. "This ignorant whipping boy knows his letters—and the royal prince can't sign his own name. Something's amiss here."

"What you thinking, Billy?" asked Cutwater.

"I'm thinking these lads have mixed themselves up to flummox us."

Jemmy lifted his chin arrogantly and tried to look as princelike as possible. "Nonsense! I'm a mere whipping boy."

The big man rumbled up a laugh, showing a mouthful of yellow teeth. "You take us for bedrock numskulls? Certain as eggs is eggs—you're the prince. The genuine, straight-up-and-down Royal Highness!"

Prince Brat's face turned red as hot iron. "That ratty street orphan?" he bellowed. "That lowborn—"

"Silence!" Jemmy commanded. "Can't you see the game is up? They're on to us. Hold your tongue!"

"But *I'm* His Royal Highness!"

Gaw! Jemmy thought. This haughty prince didn't have the sense of a gnat. Couldn't he see a plan afoot? "Save your breath!" snapped Jemmy. "Stop giving yourself airs, you witless servant boy!"

"Servant boy! Dare you address me—"

"Bag your head," snapped Hold-Your-Nose Billy. "Give him a kick, Cutwater, if we hear another peep out of him."

"Hand me the hawk's feather," said Jemmy. "I'll write my papa, the king."

CHAPTER 8
The ransom note

Hold-Your-Nose Billy tilted the princely crown on his head. "What have you writ down so far?"

Jemmy glanced up from the sheet of paper. " 'To the King's Most Sacred Majesty. Dear Papa.' "

"Aye. That sounds proper respectful. What else?"

" 'Our captors are loyal subjects, but scoundrels by trade. Don't cross them.' "

"Make that a mite stronger," said the outlaw, beginning to pace. "Tell him we're shameful mean, and rough as a sackful of nails. Warn him we fear no gallows!"

Jemmy dipped the quill in beet juice and continued scribbling. "I'll tell him you've got reserved seats in Hell."

"Aye! That's the ticket!"

Cutwater had begun gnawing away at a roasted pheasant, and his cheek swelled out as if he had a monstrous toothache. "What about the king's soldiers, Billy? Now the fog's lifted, they'll be followin' the lad like a trail of ants. Puts my spine a-shiver."

"Faw!" exclaimed Hold-Your-Nose Billy. "Even rabbits get muxxed up and lost in this forest. We're well hid, Cutwater."

"I'll warn Papa," Jemmy offered generously, "that if you spy out a single uniform, you'll crack my neck like a chicken's."

Prince Brat sat sullenly on a pile of moldy bed straw. He glared icily at the whipping boy who had seized his royal title.

"And don't forget the reward, Billy," said Cutwater. "We want the prince's weight in gold bangers, right?"

"Tell the king that," directed Hold-Your-Nose Billy. "In big letters. Now let me reckon out a safe spot to deliver the loot."

Jemmy dipped the quill, but then paused. Gaw, he thought, it's not enough to choose my words as

if I were a prince. Show some high and mighty, Jemmy. *Think* like a prince.

"Dimwits!" he flared up. "Catchpenny rogues! I will not be exchanged for such a trifle. My mere weight? A paltry treasure you could carry on a shoulder? How dare you insult me!"

Hold-Your-Nose Billy's red eyebrows shot up in bewildered surprise. "Insult you? A trifle?"

"A prince is worth a prince's ransom!"

The eyebrows lowered as quickly as they had risen. "No offense meant, lad. How would you calculate a proper ransom?"

"A wagonload of gold at the very least. And jewels mixed in."

"As I'm alive! A wagonload?"

Cutwater gulped down the wad of fowl in his mouth. "We did forget about jewels, Billy."

"A wagonload it is, then!" exclaimed the hairy outlaw.

Prince Brat's mouth fell wide open at the whipping boy's nervy mischief.

Hold-Your-Nose Billy stood over Jemmy's shoulder and watched the words being scratched out. Finally, he said, "Have you made your sign yet?"

"About to," replied Jemmy.

With as much flourish as he could manage, he wrote:

Your Obedient Son

Prince Horace

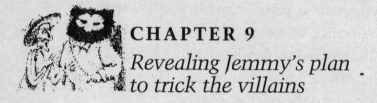

CHAPTER 9
Revealing Jemmy's plan to trick the villains

Hold-Your-Nose Billy popped a clove of garlic into his mouth, ground it between his yellow teeth, and helped himself to a veal pie. "Nothing like garlic to clear the head and fend off the plague. Cutwater, give the lads a ration of breakfast."

The scrawny outlaw sliced off two thick pieces of coarse bread. He draped a salt herring across each slice. "Eat hearty, little fellers."

"This smelly stuff!" Prince Brat glared at the bread and herring. "It's not fit for flies!"

"Why, we eat it regular, worms and all," said Cutwater, picking the bones of the pheasant.

"I'll starve first!"

"Suit yourself," Cutwater snickered. "This is the first time we've feasted off the king's own table, and there's hardly enough for me and Billy."

Jemmy sat on the bed straw beside the prince and contemplated his breakfast. He examined the bread closely, hunting for varmints. The prince, he knew, had never been starved enough to pick out wildlife from his grub.

"Eat," he whispered. "I can't find any crawly things in it."

"The bread's stale," grumbled the prince.

"Stale enough to patch a roof, but I've scoffed down worse."

The prince began to nibble around the edges. Hold-Your-Nose Billy glanced over and grinned. "Take a chaw of garlic, whipping boy. It'll improve the taste considerable."

Cutwater wiped his thin, greasy lips with the back of his hand. "Billy, how do we know the prince ain't laid a trap for us in that message? He could have said one thing and wrote another. Where'll we find someone to read it off to us?"

Jemmy lifted his chin to a regal height. "You doubt the word and honor of your prince? Insolent oafs! Curs! I'll have you horsewhipped."

Cutwater yanked Jemmy to his feet. "Who you calling them names? I'll flog your hide pink as a salmon!"

Hold-Your-Nose Billy pushed him aside. "Keep your wits. It's worse'n common murder to lay hands on a prince. No need to break any more of the king's laws than we have to. If it comes to a flogging, there's his whipping boy."

The prince's eyes widened and his face blanched white. The prospect of taking a whipping himself had never occurred to him. "But, sir, it wasn't me who called you names!"

Cutwater gave a sudden cackle. "'Sir,' is it now? That's more like it. But tell the prince here to keep a civil tongue in his head."

Prince Brat shot Jemmy a poisonous look.

The garlicky outlaw was leaning closer to Jemmy. "See here, Prince, it's not that we doubt your word and honesty. Not a bit! But all the same—let's hear you read off the message."

Jemmy turned away from the man's breath and began to read.

"No, no, lad. Let's have it from bottom to top. Read it *backwards.* I do hope for your whipping boy's sake you don't stumble and trip as if the real words ain't on paper."

Jemmy shrugged. "It says . . . 'Son Obedient Your.'"

"'Your Obedient Son,'" said Hold-Your-Nose Billy. "Keep at it."

"'Jewels and gold of cart full a of ransom a demand they."

"'They demand a ransom . . . of a cart . . . a full . . .'" The outlaw himself began to stumble and trip over the words. "Aye, that's the ticket."

Jemmy read the message through backward. And then a second time before the hairy outlaw was satisfied.

"Now then," he said. "All we got to do is get the message to the king without getting nabbed in the act."

"Simple," declared Jemmy. "Send it to the castle in the hands of my whipping boy."

CHAPTER 10

In which Prince Brat lives up to his name

Hold-Your-Nose Billy clapped a leery eye on the rat-catcher's son. "Prince, do you take me for a precious fool? Send your whipping boy! To blab out where we're hid, eh? The king will come chopping down every tree if he finds out we're nested in the forest."

Jemmy assumed a princely air of indifference. "Then tote the message yourself. It's no skin off my ear if you never get back alive." He filled his mouth with bread and herring. "I declare, this is tasty."

Prince Brat scoffed under his breath. He hadn't shown a moment's interest in Jemmy's scheme to free him. Their eyes met and clashed. Gaw, Jemmy thought, he's fuming like a stovepipe at being unprinced. He'll have me charged with treason.

"I'll stand guard over the prince," said Cutwater. "You're the one to go, Billy."

"Me?" hooted the big man. "Me, that they sing songs about, and pinch their noses? At the first whiff of garlic, it would be off with the head of Hold-Your-Nose Billy."

"Unlikely," corrected Jemmy. "True, Papa would have you tortured a mite, to loosen your tongue. But he wouldn't have your head—not Papa. He favors slow boiling in oil."

The effect on the outlaws was instant. Hold-Your-Nose Billy's jaw dropped. Sweat broke out across his face like raindrops. "Cutwater, you're skin and bones. You could slip in and out of a keyhole. I'll guard the prince."

"Faw, Billy! I don't fancy being boiled to a crisp."

The hairy outlaw gave a loud and decisive snort. "We'll send the whipping boy."

Jemmy held back a sigh of relief. "And my crown with him."

"Your golden crown?" blurted out Cutwater. "Not by half, we won't!"

Jemmy made the pretense of blazing up with impatience. "Simpleton! I swear there are not two more ignorant, cloven-footed blockheads in the land."

Prince Brat shot Jemmy a quick, thunder-scowl look. "Stop it!" he whispered harshly. "Don't give them the rough side of your tongue. You'll get me whipped!"

Jemmy ignored him. "Donkeys!" he continued.

"Before the day is out, dozens of villains will deliver up false claims. Only my crown will convince Papa that you are the genuine villain."

Hold-Your-Nose Billy began to pace, munching garlic cloves as if they were grapes. Finally, he tipped the crown off his head and flung it to Prince Brat.

"Whipping boy! Deliver it to the king! If he doesn't follow our instructions to the letter—"

"The prince'll be done for!" Cutwater snickered, drawing a knifelike finger across his throat.

"And blab all you want," added the other outlaw. "We'll pack the prince off to a different hiding place."

By its smelly tail, Prince Brat tossed aside the uneaten herring. Without showing the slightest concern for Jemmy's fate, he flicked a glance at the two outlaws. "I'll deliver nothing!" he exploded. "I won't go back to the castle!"

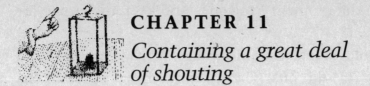

CHAPTER 11
Containing a great deal of shouting

Jemmy was struck dumb. Did Prince Brat have sand for brains? Gaw! Didn't he realize he could snatch up his crown and go free?

"It doesn't please me to take orders from common rascals," Prince Brat said coldly.

"It would please me to shake the teeth out of your confounded face!" replied Hold-Your-Nose Billy. "You may live in the castle, but you're only a whipping boy. Do as we say!"

"I'll do what I choose. And I choose not to run your errands."

Jemmy leaped up and gave the prince an angry flash of eyes. "Jemmy-From-The-Streets gets these stubborn fits," he said. "Contrary as a mule! Let me have a word with him."

"I'll whip the mulishness out of him!" exclaimed Cutwater, lurching forward.

Prince Brat dodged out of his grasp, and a sour smile crossed his face. "I'll tear up your vile message the moment I'm gone. And keep the crown for myself!"

Hold-Your-Nose Billy caught Cutwater's upraised arm. "Hold off! There's something in what he says."

"You think he's angling for a share of the reward, Billy?"

"Likely is."

"The greedy little snipe," Cutwater bleated. "How much do you reckon we can spare?"

"This calls for private words. Let's parley. Follow me."

The moment the outlaws ducked out of the hut, Jemmy turned on his companion.

"Prince Blockhead! You should wear your crown to fend off woodpeckers."

"Imposter! How dare you insult me!"

"You're enough to give the devil himself fits! Haven't I so muddled their brains they want to turn you loose? And you reward me with a royal squawk!"

The prince had crossed to the wicker basket and snatched up an uneaten apple tart. He gobbled it down.

"I'll return to the castle when I'm ready. When *I* choose. And not a moment before!"

Jemmy's eyes narrowed sharply. He couldn't fathom what was stirring in the prince's mind. Could he, for once, be concerned for someone other than himself? "It's not *me* you think you're protecting, is it?"

"You?"

"Knowing they'll knock the daylights out of me soon as they find out I tricked them?"

The prince shrugged. "You're quick, boy. You'll think of something."

"I've already thought it. Once you're up and gone, I'll slip away. Out in the forest, I'll be harder to catch than a flea."

"But I'm not leaving," said the prince firmly.

"Gaw! But why? Is it your pa you're afraid of? Is that why you won't go back?"

The prince scoffed. "He won't miss me."

"'Course he will!"

"Let him wait. And mind your own affairs, whipping boy."

"It *is* my affair. Do you reckon you're out on a lark? With murderers outside?"

The murderers shuffled back into the hut. Hold-Your-Nose Billy fixed Prince Brat with a hairy smile. "Never let it be sung about that me and Cutwater ain't generous to a fault, lad. We'll share out with you a bucketful of gold and jewels!"

"No," replied the prince flatly, as if he'd been offered a bucketful of coal.

"Don't run me out of patience!" warned the huge outlaw.

The prince remained defiant. "I'm staying."

Hold-Your-Nose Billy ripped off his leather belt. "I'll lash a bit of sense into your head!"

Jemmy saw that Prince Brat wasn't going to shift his ground. "You don't need my whipping boy to get into the castle. There's a better way."

"Do say!" exclaimed Cutwater doubtfully.

"My horse," remarked Jemmy. "There's your messenger, sirs!"

Hold-Your-Nose Billy gave a snort. "Faw! That fine beast? We've been afoot since our skin-poor horse turned heels up. We need a mount in our line of work."

"Nitwits!" exclaimed Jemmy, as if his own princely patience were at an end. "With rings on your fingers and gold in your pockets, you can take to the roads like gentlemen. You'll be traveling about in fine coaches. But first you've got to lay hands on the treasure."

Cutwater made a sound through his nose like a pitchpipe. "With that horse outside?"

"One of the king's own. A horse can always find his way home, can't it? That fine beast will make for the castle stables, note and crown. No questions asked!"

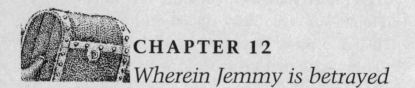

CHAPTER 12
Wherein Jemmy is betrayed

With a gleeful chuckle, Hold-Your-Nose Billy dropped the ransom note and the golden crown into a dirty linen sack.

When he'd knotted the sack to the saddle, he turned to Cutwater. "Soon as I'm within a squint of the castle, I'll turn the beast loose. Guard our prisoners!"

"I'll tie 'em up," Cutwater wheezed, giving his heavy partner a foot up into the royal saddle.

From the doorway, Jemmy watched Hold-Your-Nose Billy vanish into the tangled maze of tree limbs and brambles. Then he glanced about at the bare furnishings, the hanging ropes of garlic bulbs, the bed straw, the chest of stolen goods. He'd need some trickery to escape.

The prince fixed him with a smirk. "You're clever, all right. But a common dunce all the same."

"Gaw."

"A cartload of gold and jewels! The ruffians would have been content with a mere jingle of coins."

Jemmy's eyes swung back to the bed straw.

There was his escape!

"A cartload o' moonshine," he said. "It'll never be forked over."

"I'm the prince! Papa will have to pay it!"

Jemmy began burrowing like a barn mouse under the moldy straw. "Not a bit, he won't."

"Papa will foam at the mouth!"

Jemmy was disappearing, limb by limb, under the straw. "Think again. It'll be clear as water the note's a scrambly-witted fake."

"Papa'll keep me under lock and key after this!"

"It won't fool a soul, that note. How could you have written it? Everyone in the castle knows you can't so much as sign your own name."

"I never needed to before!"

"It's me that's in the soup. I'll catch it for your mischief in running away. And I'll catch it again when the tutor claps eyes on the handwriting. He'll say, 'Jemmy! This is Jemmy trying to line his own pockets.' Your pa'll scrag me with his bare hands! So I'll be obliged if you'd help me nip out o' here."

"I promise you my protection," announced the prince with sudden generosity.

"Jemmy protects himself," said the whipping boy. "When that plaguy Cutwater comes to tie us up, tell him I slipped out the door. Soon as he bounces off after me, I'll make a break for it."

"You'd leave me alone with cutthroats?"

Before Jemmy could answer, he heard the sharp squeak of the door. He held his breath.

"Lads, you won't mind if I truss you up like a Christmas goose."

There came a sudden pause, and Jemmy's heart began to thump.

"Where's the prince?" Cutwater snapped.

Jemmy heard Prince Brat answer without the slightest hesitation.

"Him? Over there. Under the straw."

CHAPTER 13
The chase

A thoroughbred of the streets, Jemmy acted on instinct. He didn't wait to be nabbed.

In a burst of straw, he shot up and made a leap for the door. Cutwater, startled, lost the merest breath of time. But it was enough.

Jemmy flung open the door and ran.

His long arms outstretched, Cutwater lurched after him.

And Prince Brat followed.

Jemmy vanished into the wild green tangle. He jumped a great fallen log, ducked under low-hanging branches, and, like a rabbit, made sudden changes in direction.

He could hear Cutwater close behind, breathing like a bellows. "I'm on your tracks! Stop before I get aggravexed with you, Prince!"

Jemmy covered the ground at full tilt. Leaves crackled under his feet. Gaw! he thought. He might as well be leading a confounded parade, for all the noise he was making.

He reached a small clearing—and half jumped out of his skin. Sniffing near the skeleton-white roots of an upturned hollow tree stood a wild beast.

A bear!

Jemmy would have preferred Cutwater's own company. But before he could find his legs, the hairy beast took flight.

It went crashing away to Jemmy's left.

Jemmy got his breath back. Then, almost without thinking, he dove into the hollow of the dead tree and snugged himself in.

Moments later he caught the merest glimpse of Cutwater cupping an ear. Turning on his heels, the rattleboned man gave a shout. "Practically got you by the hind leg, pesky Prince!"

Jemmy let out a small sigh of relief. Cutwater would have a mighty surprise if he caught that bear by the hind leg.

As the sounds of the chase grew fainter, Jemmy crawled out of the hollow root. The sun was now high enough to send down smoky rays of light through the treetops. Which way was the river?

And then he saw Prince Brat, his face lobster-red from running, at the edge of the clearing.

"Unfaithful servant!" he protested, glaring hard at Jemmy.

Until this moment, Jemmy hadn't had a moment's pause for anger. But now fury shot into his eyes. Curse this blabber-tongued, hateful prince! "You betrayed me!"

"You'd have deserted me without a care!"

Jemmy bristled. "Ain't it me they think is the prince? If you hadn't pointed me out under the straw, Cutwater would have flown off to pick up my tracks. And we could have crept away dead easy. I wouldn't be running my lungs out!"

The prince pondered this for a moment. He nodded. "Then I forgive you."

Jemmy was speechless for a moment. "Forgive me! Don't trouble yourself, my good and loyal Prince. And get yourself another whipping boy."

"But I have not dismissed you from my service," said the prince calmly.

"I dismiss myself," Jemmy fired back. "I'll get where I'm going, and you can find your own way back to the castle."

"I'll go with you."

"Not likely!"

Jemmy turned to the right and beat his way back into the foliage.

CHAPTER 14

*In which is heard
a voice in the forest*

Jemmy could hear Prince Brat following in his tracks, step by step. He grimly pressed on.

Brambles, reaching out like cat's claws, tore at their fine garments. The forest trees rose all around them like prison bars.

Finally, Jemmy spun around. "Lay off! Go your own way!"

"This way suits me," said the prince.

"Well, don't follow me. I've no more idea than a gnat where I'm headin'."

"Silence," whispered the prince, with a turn of his head. "Hear that?"

They froze, the two of them.

A voice came wailing through the woods.

"Tunia! Pet-Pet-Petunia!"

And then a young woman appeared, barefoot and jangling with bracelets. She moved through the trees as quickly as a wood spirit.

"Pet-Pet-Petunia!"

She carried a coiled rope in one hand and held

outstretched in the other an amber chunk of comb honey.

"Come here, darlin'! Come to Betsy."

Suddenly, as if sensing a presence in the trees, she headed toward Jemmy and the prince.

"Petunia? You there, naughty rascal! Smell the honey? Come feast yourself, Pet!"

Jemmy didn't know what to make of this woman—girl, really. For as she drew closer, he reckoned she couldn't be more than fourteen or fifteen years old. He stepped out into full view, with the prince clinging to him like a shadow.

"Miss?"

She stopped short. "My eyes! Who are you?"

"Lost," said Jemmy. "Would you know which way to the river?"

"'Course I do. Ain't we headin' for the fair, me and Petunia? Have you seen him?"

"Petunia?"

"Got loose, he did! My dancing bear. World famous!"

"Scared me out of my skin," Jemmy replied, and pointed. "Back there."

She turned on her heels and started off.

"Hey!" Jemmy shouted. "Where's the river!"

"Where it's always been. Due south!"

"Which way is south?"

Betsy paused to set her arm like a signpost. "Straight on!"

"You certain?"

"Certain I'm certain. Didn't Pa always say I had a head like a compass, rest him in peace!"

And she was gone.

Their clothes were ripped to tatters by late morning when Jemmy and the prince caught sight of the sparkling river. And almost at once they dove back into cover.

Mounted on high-stepping horses, a pair of soldiers were advancing along the river road.

"They must be out searching for you," Jemmy whispered. "If they catch me with you, I'm done for!"

Prince Brat didn't seem to be listening. His eyes were fixed on the passing soldiers.

"Look here," Jemmy muttered impatiently. "I can't have you sticking to me like a barnacle. Ain't you had a snoutful o' running away? Go back with the soldiers!"

The prince shook his head. "Let them pass." And

then he added with the faintest of smiles, "This is the first time no one has had fits because I got my clothes grimy. The ladies keep me clean and starched as a pillowcase!"

"But you're a prince!"

"Is my face dirty as yours?"

"You don't belong knockin' about outside the walls!"

Prince Brat gazed off into the distance. "Did you have lots of friends when you lived on the streets?"

"Heaps."

"Heaps—of course."

"And hardly a one of 'em wouldn't fight me over a bone. Go back. Your pa must be having double fits o' worry."

The prince answered with a flash of resentment. "I might as well be stuffed and hung on the wall like a stag's head—for all he notices me."

"You remind him often enough, with all your pranks. How long are you going to let him sweat and stew?"

"I don't know," declared the prince. "Maybe I'll never go back. This is the best time I ever had!"

"Gaw," Jemmy murmured.

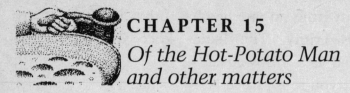

CHAPTER 15
Of the Hot-Potato Man and other matters

The soldiers had passed by.

Following the river, Jemmy ventured toward the city. Prince Brat strode along beside him.

"Soon as I can, I aim to give you the slip," Jemmy warned. "You'll be on your own."

The prince said nothing.

The tide was low and they traveled out of sight of the road, below a grassy embankment. In the distance, against billowing white clouds, stood a jackstraw jumble of ships' masts.

"You *can* fend for your own self, can't you?" Jemmy asked suddenly.

"Of course I can!" answered the prince in a stinging voice. "I don't need flocks of servants to fetch and carry for me."

"It's settled, then."

"Settled! Skip off anytime you like."

With the tide out, a wide mud flat lay exposed. From long habit, Jemmy kept his eyes peeled for treasure. Sandpipers scattered like mice before him.

He spotted a barrel stave and pounced upon it.

"Trash," remarked the prince. "What are you doing?"

"Mudlarking."

"What?"

"I've got to eat, don't I? If I can collect enough driftwood, I can sell it as firewood."

The prince shrugged and walked on ahead. Jemmy gazed after him for a moment. What did a prince know about living off the streets? His meals had always appeared on China plates and silver trays as if by magic. Left to himself, he'd starve.

"It's not my worry," Jemmy muttered.

"What?"

"You, that's what. If you get hungry enough, you'll scramble back to the castle."

The prince glared back at Jemmy, and then stooped down to retrieve the broken leg of a chair from the mud. "Is this worth anything?"

Jemmy nodded. Before long, the two of them had collected three more barrel staves and the back of the chair.

Then Jemmy found something even more valuable to him—a bent and battered birdcage. He could go into business with that! Straightened out, it would hold rats.

They rounded a bend and the crack of a whip sounded in the air like a firecracker. Jemmy crawled up the embankment for a look.

A weary old coach was mired in a mudhole on the road. The coachman, looking just as old and rickety, held the reins of his two-horse team and cracked his whip in the air again.

"Pull, gents! Be good lads! It's me own fault, not leadin' you around this bog. Me eyesight ain't what it was, is it, old tars?"

Jemmy watched for another moment as the horses tried to pull the coach free. The coach was enameled blue, with yellow lettering painted on the door panel:

Capt. Harry Nips

HOT-POTATO MAN

Jemmy crawled over the embankment. A ride to the city would suit him fine.

"Sir? Would you take on a passenger? Here, let me set these barrel staves under the wheels."

"Don't mind if you do," said Captain Nips. "I'm late for the fair as it is."

Jemmy busied himself, laying a firm track for the wheels. Prince Brat watched from the edge of the embankment.

"You must be carrying a heavy load," Jemmy cried out. "Try again, Cap'n!"

The old man cracked his whip, the horses strained—and the coach rolled up out of the bog.

"Hop in, lad."

Jemmy opened the door and saw that the coach was heavily loaded with raw potatoes and a huge iron kettle. Jemmy settled himself as best he could, and the coach lurched forward.

At last, Jemmy thought, you're free of the prince! But he couldn't resist a backward glance.

Prince Brat was standing in the center of the road. He'd dropped his load of driftwood and merely gazed at the receding coach.

Jemmy straightened, and folded his arms. The prince wasn't his lookout any longer. But he'd stood there like a wounded bird. Blast him! A prince hadn't a cockeyed notion how to fend for himself.

"Stop, Cap'n!" Jemmy shouted. "We left me friend behind."

The hot-potato man pulled up on the reins. Jemmy leaned out a window. With an arm he motioned Prince Brat to come along.

For an instant, Jemmy thought he saw a smile flash across the prince's face. But it had vanished by the time the heir to the throne joined him inside the coach.

They rode in silence. Jemmy wondered what had possessed him to refer to Prince Brat as his friend. Friend? Cows would give beer first!

Then, minutes later, the coach rocked to a sudden halt.

"Stand and deliver!" came a shout.

A pair of highwaymen were training pistols on Captain Nips. Jemmy hardly had to peer out. The voice was familiar.

It was Hold-Your-Nose Billy. And Cutwater.

 **CHAPTER 16**
Wherein the prince neither bawls nor bellows

Jemmy felt a surge of the creeps.

Run for it? he wondered. Instead, he began to burrow out of sight under the loose heap of potatoes. "Remember," he whispered to the prince, "it's me they're after, not you. Tell 'em we split up. Tell 'em I swam the river."

Prince Brat merely looked at him.

The voices outside boomed.

"Stand and deliver, I said!"

"And I heard you," exclaimed Captain Nips. "Deliver what? Potatoes? Scurvy rascals! Help yourselves."

"Hang your potatoes!" roared Hold-Your-Nose Billy. "Deliver us some information and you can be off. We're after two runaway apprentices."

"Apprentice highwaymen?" Captain Nips scoffed.

"Our affair. Girl with a bear said she saw 'em streakin' for the river. You carryin' passengers?"

Jemmy pulled the iron kettle over his head.

A coach door was yanked open, and Jemmy could hear Cutwater's muffled cackle.

"Got one! The whipping boy, it is! Where's your master, eh?"

Jemmy held his breath. He had no reason to believe that the prince wouldn't betray him again.

There came a stiff pause.

And then Prince Brat said, "Swam the river."

By then Hold-Your-Nose Billy had ripped open the opposite coach door. Even through the kettle Jemmy imagined he could smell garlic.

"Swimmed the river! Faw! He'd need scales and fins."

Hardly a moment later, the kettle was grabbed off and Jemmy's head stood exposed.

"Here's the potato we're after!" Hold-Your-Nose Billy roared gleefully.

Jemmy and the prince were yanked out of the coach, and the big outlaw shouted to Captain Nips, "Throw me down your horsewhip, and drive on!"

Hanging on to each boy by the scruff of the neck, the highwaymen scrambled out of sight below the embankment.

Hold-Your-Nose Billy looked angry enough to throttle Jemmy on the spot.

"Tricked me, did you!" he bellowed. "Flummoxed me with your fancy quill-scratchin'!"

The game's up, Jemmy thought. He's tumbled that the ransom note ain't worth scat. But, trying to look as innocent as possible, he replied, "Sir?"

"A gold sack or two would have satisfied me and Cutwater," snarled the hairy outlaw. "Greedy ain't our middle name. But you! Raising the ante to a great cartload! Reckoned to slow us down, didn't you? It would be easier to drag around a dead horse! If we ain't lightfooted, we're caught. That was your scheme!"

What a pair of fools, Jemmy thought. That hadn't

been his scheme at all! "You've got it all wrong," he declared. "I swear it!"

"Aye, enough plunder to burden us directly to the gallows, eh?" Hold-Your-Nose Billy continued. "Well, here's a whipping you won't never forget!"

He snapped Captain Nip's whip in the air to get the feel of it.

"Here's the whipping boy," Cutwater put in. "You said it'll go powerful worse for us if we thrash the prince himself."

Hold-Your-Nose Billy nodded sharply. Cutwater upturned the prince, holding him by the ankles in the air. "Go to it, Billy."

Jemmy finally found his voice. "Lay down the whip," he commanded with a princely air. "Don't you have an ounce of sense between you?"

"Hold your gab!"

"Simpletons! You can just fill your pockets with plunder and be lightfooted as ever," Jemmy declared.

"Nobody flummoxes Hold-Your-Nose Billy and gets away with it!"

The whip snapped across the prince's back.

Jemmy held his breath. He knew what it felt like. He saw that Prince Brat had set his jaws, just as

Jemmy had always done—and not a sound escaped his lips.

"Harder!" Cutwater advised. "You didn't raise a peep out of him."

The big man let fly again.

"He must have a hide like an elephant," said Cutwater. "He don't feel a thing."

"He'll feel this!" Hold-Your-Nose Billy thundered, and the leather whistled through the air. The prince's jacket was being shredded.

"Bawl out!" Jemmy shouted. He'd dreamed of seeing the prince whipped, but now that it was happening he found no satisfaction in it. "Holler and cry out! I won't tell anyone!"

But Prince Brat only girded himself for the next blow.

From the top of the embankment came an outraged voice. Betsy and her dancing bear stood there.

"Ruffian!" she cried out. "What are you doing to that poor boy?"

"No business of yours," snarled Cutwater.

"Stop it!"

But Hold-Your-Nose Billy raised the whip again. The next thing Jemmy knew, the girl had slipped the rope from around the bear's neck.

"Sic 'em, Petunia! Go get 'em!"

CHAPTER 17
Petunia to the rescue

The bear came snarling down the embankment.

Rising on its hind legs, it bared its teeth and bellowed out a thunderclap of a roar.

Cutwater dropped the prince and was off like a greyhound. Hold-Your-Nose Billy, his eyes round as snowballs, went charging off into the river. He raised a great splash, and if he didn't know how to swim, he learned—instantly.

Jemmy had reared back, but now Betsy gave a whistle and the bear stopped in its tracks.

"Good boy, Petunia! That'll do, darlin'." She slipped the rope back around the bear's neck. Then she bent over the prince. "The lowdown bullies! Laying stripes on a boy's back!"

With the bear sniffing him, Prince Brat didn't move a muscle. "Rein in your beast," he whispered stiffly.

"Oh, don't be afraid of Petunia. Gentle as a kitten, he is. Here, let me tend to your poor hide."

"No."

"Give us a look."

"Thank you, no!" the prince exclaimed.

"Lumme! Ain't you the brave one! Must sting something dreadful."

Jemmy watched the prince slowly raise himself off the mud flat. He felt a growing amazement. Prince Brat a brave one? It didn't seem possible. But gaw! There was a cast-iron streak of pluck in him.

The prince moved his arms and shoulders. He winced, but then began to brush himself off.

"Steady on your legs?" Jemmy asked.

"Steady."

"You should have yelled and bellowed. That's what they wanted to hear."

"And humble myself?" muttered the prince. "*You* never did."

Jemmy gazed at him for a thoughtful moment. Then he indicated the two highwaymen. Cutwater had vanished, and Hold-Your-Nose Billy was trying to keep from drowning. "Let's be on our way. They're sure to be back after us."

"Not if you travel with me," said Betsy. "Me and Petunia."

Jemmy found the horsewhip where Hold-Your-Nose Billy had dropped it. Betsy and the bear had already started up the embankment, and the boys followed.

"Lawks," whispered Jemmy. "Ain't we a puckered sight, the both of us! Torn up and scruffy. At least, no one'll take you for a prince."

Not far off lay the coach on its side.

"Hanged if I caught sight of that steep rise off to the side of the road," explained Captain Nips. "Tipped us over, as you see."

"Either your horses need spectacles," said Betsy, "or you do."

Together with Petunia, they lifted and pushed and righted the coach. They piled in and were off.

Betsy and her dancing bear rode inside with the prince. Jemmy decided to sit with Captain Nips to watch for road hazards.

They reached the city without further incident, except for being stopped by soldiers. The king's men were clearly looking for the vanished prince, but when a bear poked its head out the door window, the soldiers stepped back and quickly waved the coach on.

CHAPTER 18

*Of assorted events in which
the plot thickens thicker*

As soon as the wheels rattled on cobbled streets, Jemmy felt an immense sense of relief. This was his turf, the city, and he knew more places to hide than a rat.

Approaching the waterside fairgrounds, he saw prisoners in chains being marched aboard a convict ship. It lay in sharp contrast to the festive stalls and banners of the fair.

Captain Nips eased the coach between a seller of live fowl and a juggler tossing colored balls into the bright noonday air.

"Thanks for the jolly ride, hot-potato man," said Betsy. "Come along, Petunia. Let's fetch us a crowd and earn a copper or two."

Jemmy collected his battered birdcage.

"Don't rush off, lad," said Captain Nips, hauling out a canvas load of firewood from under the seat. "Ain't I been listening to your stomach rumbling-bumbling for the last hour? Do me the kindness of filling the kettle at the pump. Soon as the potatoes are boiled up, we'll feast, eh?"

Anxious as he was to be on his way, Jemmy hesitated. He *was* powerful hungry.

Then Captain Nips laid a coin in his hand. "And while you're at it, stop off at the cow lady, the both of you, and get yourselves a couple of mugs to drink."

Jemmy picked up the handle of the kettle. But almost at once Prince Brat snatched it out of his hands. "I'll do that."

"You?" Jemmy replied. "It's servant's work."

"Then who'd take me for a prince, toting water?" He smiled. He laughed. "I've never been allowed to carry anything! Not in my entire life."

Jemmy led the way. He'd never regarded fetching and carrying as a privilege. Princes and such-like were hard to fathom! But the sound of merriment lingered in his head. He'd never before heard Prince Brat laugh.

They dodged acrobats and a stilt walker and a harp player. Through the hubbub came a great squeaky voice.

"Jemmy! Rat-catchin' Jemmy!"

Turning, Jemmy spied a tall boy wearing a checked cap. It was Smudge tending a sawdust pit squared off by a board fence—a dog-and-rat pit. Beside him stood a stack of rat-filled cages and a black terrier leashed to a post.

"By gigs, it *is* you, Jemmy!" said Smudge. "Reckon you call the king by his first name these days."

"Hello, Smudge. You give up mudlarking?"

"I've come up in the world, ain't I? Same as you, Jemmy. How do you like me dog? Best rat-fighter you ever saw."

With a practiced eye, Jemmy surveyed the cages. "But those rats look tame enough to eat off your hand."

"Best I could afford. Catch me some castle rats and I'll make a special feature. The king's own rats!"

"Not my line o' work in the castle, Smudge."

"It's not true you're whipping boy, is it?"

Jemmy felt a flush of embarrassment and dodged the question. "I've learned to read and write."

"Naw!"

"The bottom truth. I've read many a book from beginning to end."

"What's in 'em?"

"All nature o' things. I can do sums, too."

Smudge was impressed. "Ain't that a wonder! I never heard of a rat-catcher could read and write and do sums. It don't fit. Don't forget your old friends when you grow up to be duke or something."

"I aim to go back to the sewers," replied Jemmy stiffly. "I'll catch you some rats first chance."

But even as he said it, Jemmy felt a bleak discomfort. He would miss the shelves of books he'd left behind in the castle. In the sewers, he hadn't been aware of his own ignorance. He saw no choice now but to return. But he realized that he'd lost his taste for ignorance.

Smudge was saying, "Who's the cove?"

"What?"

"Your pal."

"This is—" Jemmy caught himself. He began to stammer. "I mean, this is—"

The prince answered for him. "Friend-O'-Jemmy's the name."

"Then Friend-O'-Jemmy'll do." Smudge put out his hand to shake.

Jemmy caught Prince Brat's momentary confusion. "He never shakes hands."

"Of course I do," said the prince with a quick grin. He took Smudge's hand. "Glad to shake your hand, Smudge."

"Likewise."

And Jemmy dragged the prince away. Smudge had committed a terrible offense: no one was allowed to shake hands with a prince. "Why did you do that?"

"Because I've never shaken hands before."

"He could be hung for less!"

The prince was staring at his hand. "It felt friendly . . . trusting. I may introduce the practice at court when I become king."

Jemmy's ears pricked up. King, is it? he thought. So it was just bluster that you might never go back to the castle. Gaw, I hope you don't want to learn to catch rats first.

Moments later they came to a stout old woman with hands as gnarled as tree roots. Beside her, munching grass, stood a cow with a brass ring in its nose.

"New milk!" the cow lady called out. "New milk, fresh from the cow! Best in the land! New milk!"

Jemmy handed over the coin. The milk lady fished two mugs out of a tub of water, sat on a stool, and began to milk the cow directly into the mugs. Her aim was as skilled as an archer's.

"Have you heard the earful?" she asked. "Our prince has been abducticated. Imagine!"

"Imagine," the prince replied coolly. She was looking directly at him.

"Our darlin' poor king!" she went on. "Weepin' his royal eyes out, no doubt. Though why he'd spring a tear for the little toad, I don't know. A mighty terror, they say, is Prince Brat. Pity us the day *he* becomes king, eh?"

She handed over the pair of mugs. Jemmy drank the warm milk down in unbroken gulps. But then he noticed the prince standing motionless, a vague, unseeing look in his eyes. For certain he knew everyone called him Prince Brat behind his back, didn't he?

"Drink up, lad," said the cow lady. "My stars, I've never seen such rags on a boy. They look like castoffs from the old-clothes man." She gave out a joking laugh. "Drink up before you scare off business."

The prince drained the mug and shuffled away.

As they filled the potato kettle at the pump, he looked at Jemmy. "Treasonous old woman. I could have her tongue ripped off for lying."

But there was no steam in his voice. Taking a whipping was bad enough, but to learn that his subjects dreaded the day he'd grow up and become king had deeply shaken him.

"She meant no harm," Jemmy murmured, keeping his eyes alert for soldiers.

"Is that what they call me—Prince Brat?"

Jemmy nodded.

"Does everyone hate me?"

"More'n likely."

"What about you?"

Jemmy hesitated for a moment. "I did. But maybe I don't." Jemmy couldn't sort out his feelings. "The pot's full. Let's go."

It took the two of them to carry the iron kettle, now full of water. They passed a magician with a bald head, a street fiddler, and an umbrella seller, his wares opened around his feet like black silken mushrooms. Suddenly there loomed up a soldier on horseback, his eyes on the search.

There was nothing to do but brazen it out. Jemmy took a tighter grip on the handle, but was ready to fly if he had to. The soldier passed by with only the merest glance.

What was he looking for, a prince in fine velvets and a crown cocked on his head? Was it clothes that made a prince, Jemmy wondered, just as rags made a street boy? He had a notion that the prince felt secretly disappointed not to be recognized by any of his subjects. Wasn't he getting his head stuffed with surprises!

Before long, potatoes were boiling in the pot. Not far off, Betsy had drawn a crowd with Petunia, now balancing a gentleman's hat on his nose. And then the bear began passing the hat for tips.

Jemmy no longer felt the slightest concern about the soldiers. He had no doubt that Hold-Your-Nose Billy would trace him and the prince to the fair. Hadn't they fallen into the company of a girl with a trained bear? Where else would she be going?

Finally, Captain Nips began spearing boiled potatoes, and Betsy returned with Petunia.

"We could eat a bushel!" she exclaimed, jingling a handful of coins.

"Courtesy to fellow artistes," said Captain Nips, refusing the money. He split open a pair of plump potatoes. "Salt and pepper?"

"Pepper for me, salt for Petunia."

Captain Nips reached into one coat pocket for a pinch of salt, and into the other for pepper.

"Salt for me," said Jemmy.

"And you?" Captain Nips asked the prince.

The heir to the throne balked for a moment, and Jemmy knew why. He'd certainly never eaten a po-

tato before. In the castle, roots were regarded as peasant food. "I—I don't know," the prince stammered.

"When in doubt, salt," chuckled Captain Nips. And then he began calling out to the passing crowd: "Hot-hot-hot potatoes! Captain Nips' hot-hot potatoes!"

Jemmy gorged himself, anxious to be off and not certain when he would eat again. The prince nibbled at first, with his fingers, and then threw his royal pride to the winds. He bit off whole mouthfuls.

A ballad seller was working his way through the crowd, crying out his wares. He waved a bamboo pole with long paper streamers fluttering from the tip.

"Three yards of songs, a copper! Old songs, new songs! Sing 'em yourself! Ten verses of 'Poor Pitiful Polly'—will make you weep! Sixteen verses of that notable highwayman Hold-Your-Nose Billy!"

Jemmy's ears pricked up as the ballad seller began singing a sample of his merchandise.

> "Hold-Your-Nose Billy, a wild man is he,
> Hang him from a gallows tree.
> Here he comes, there he goes:
> Don't forget to hold your nose."

The street song had once amused Jemmy. But now he only sharpened his eyes.

He wiped his hands on his sleeves and turned to Captain Nips. "Thanks for the grub, sir."

"Where are you off to?" asked Betsy. "Here's the place to put a jingle in your pockets. Can't you turn cartwheels or something?"

"I catch rats," Jemmy said simply.

"Rats?" Betsy made a face. "What on earth for?"

"There's good money in sewer rats. The meaner, the better."

"My eyes!" exclaimed Betsy. "Don't you get bit?"

"Many a time," said Jemmy.

Captain Nips cocked an ear. "What's that running patterer yelling about?"

A crowlike voice pierced the air. And then the news seller appeared, his tongue wagging like a bell clapper, a bundle of broadsides under his arm.

"PRINCE SOLD TO GYPSIES! THE TRUE AND GENUINE FACTS! INK STILL WET! WHIPPING BOY CHARGED WITH DASTARDLY SCHEME! KING OFFERS REWARD FOR THE UNSPEAKABLE RASCAL! DEAD OR ALIVE! FULL DESCRIPTION! GET YOUR COPY! KEEP YOUR EYES PEELED AND CATCH THE REWARD!"

The running patterer was selling his broadsides almost as fast as he could yell.

The facts were cockeyed, but Jemmy grabbed his birdcage, backed off—and was gone.

CHAPTER 19

*Being a full account
of the happenings
in the dark sewers*

Jemmy headed for the only safe place he knew—the sewers. He scrambled along the docks.

And the prince dogged him every step of the way.

Jemmy turned on him like a cornered rat. "Ain't you done enough? You've got a price put on my head! Go home, and go to blazes!"

"But you're my friend," the prince stated, as if he were issuing a royal decree.

"Don't count on it!" replied Jemmy.

He started down stone steps to the river, but the prince stopped him with a sudden, urgent yelp. "Look!"

Looming up on the cobbled wayside came the

hulk of Hold-Your-Nose Billy, with Cutwater following as close as a cow's tail.

Jemmy didn't wait to be spotted. But it was too late. The big outlaw, his hair and beard looking bonfire red under the bright sun, gave a distant yell and altered course.

Jemmy and the prince took the stairs in leaps. The tide was coming in and the mud flat had shrunk to the width of a path.

Jemmy led the way through a tarred forest of wharf pilings and over a derelict river barge. He leaped off into shallow water. He could already see the great brick mouth of a main sewer.

"Don't leave footprints in the mud!" he warned.

They splashed along the water's edge—and were there.

The arched sewer stood tall enough for a horse and rider. Jemmy leaped the mud and was in.

But the prince balked. "It's black as night in there!"

"Jump! Quick!"

The prince steeled himself and made the leap. Jemmy advanced into the tunnel, but the prince held back.

"Follow me! We'll be lucky if they didn't catch sight of us!"

The prince stood terrified of the darkness ahead. He had turned dead white.

Jemmy made a grab and yanked the prince after him. "You'll get me caught!"

"I'm—I'm scared, Jemmy!"

"Don't fret about the dark! There are rats in here. Even grown men are scared of 'em! Hang on to me."

Deeper and deeper, darker and darker, they sloshed through the cavernous sewer. The gutters of the city overhead had dried, but old rain seeped and dripped from the glazed brick walls.

Soon the mouth had receded to little more than a pinhole of light, and Jemmy stopped to catch his breath. "Blacker'n a stack of black cats in here, ain't it? We should come to another passage before long. They'll never find us. Ease off my arm! You'll break it."

"Jemmy." Hardly above a breath, the prince's voice was stiff with fear.

Jemmy? Not Jemmy-From-The-Streets? Not boy? The wonder of it. Jemmy thought. Like we was old knockabout friends of the streets.

"I wish I were like you," muttered the prince.

Jemmy was amazed. "Like *me*!"

"You're not afraid of anything."

"'Course I am. I'm afraid your pa'll hang me!"

"Not likely."

Jemmy gave a small snort. "Not likely, unless you give away my hiding place down here."

"Do you think I'd do that, Jemmy?"

"I don't know. Let's keep moving."

As they edged along the wet walls, Jemmy gave his reply a second thought. He'd wronged the prince. This wasn't the same Prince Brat who'd run away the night before, bored with his own meanness and haughtiness and cruelty. "Reckon I do trust you," said Jemmy.

And the prince replied, "I won't go back to the castle unless you go with me."

"Gaw!"

The main sewer branched off, and Jemmy had to stop to get his bearings. Careful, he thought. That passage to the left leads to the brewery. You could get eaten alive! Keep to the right branch.

In the hollowness of the sewer there came a soft scurring of feet, and then a distinct squeaking sound. The prince's fingers locked on Jemmy's arm like a manacle.

"Nothing but a rat," Jemmy said. "Two of 'em. But nothing to worry about yet. Dark ain't so bad if you know what's in it. Like off to the left. So hang on to me."

The prince's voice was almost inaudible. "What's to the left?"

"A brewery overhead. They empty their used-up grain down the sewer, and the rats feed and breed by the hundreds. Grow big as street cats. And short-tempered! They'll swarm all over you and hang on by their teeth."

Still clinging to the birdcage, Jemmy continued feeling his way along. He wondered how he'd ever felt at home in these dank, smelly sewers. Then a sudden flicker of light from a side passage stopped him. He peered down the tunnel and saw a figure with a candle fixed to the stiff bill of his cap. A rat-catcher! He could see a cage full of squealing rats.

He entered the passage, and the man looked up. "Who goes there?"

"Didn't mean to give you a scare," Jemmy whispered.

"This is no place for boys!"

The man's full voice boomed and echoed through the sewers, and Jemmy took a quick look behind.

"Hold it down, sir!" he said softly. And then he thought he recognized the rat-catcher. "Ain't you Ol' Johnny Tosher?"

With the candle glowing from his hat bill, the man bent forward.

"I declare! Is that you, Jemmy?"

"It is."

"Ain't you grown since you left the sewers!"

"I'd be obliged if you'd snuff out your candle, sir. There's bloodthirsty ruffians after us."

"Speak up," said the old man, cupping a hand to his ear. "Is it true you've got taken up by the king himself? That's the gossip. What are you doin' back in the sewers?"

"Running for our lives!"

"Eh?"

"Your candle'll give us away."

"What's that?"

"You'd do us a kindness to pinch it out."

"Speak up, lad. Now you're a king's little gentleman, they learn you to talk in whispers? Come back for a visit, have you! Oh, your pa'd be proud." He gave the top of Jemmy's head a pat. "They say you're Prince Brat's own whipping boy." Suddenly the rat-catcher straightened. "Who's there?"

Looming up in the yellow glow stood an immense hairy figure and a rattleboned man.

Jemmy's heart stopped cold.

"What the blazes!" roared Hold-Your-Nose Billy.

"They flummoxed us, Cutwater! That one ain't the prince! It's the other!"

"I heard!" Cutwater cried out. "We whipped the prince himself! Worse'n common murder, you said!"

"Aye, the king'll skin us alive by inches!"

"Mercy on us!"

"But not if he don't find out!"

Both lurched forward to grab the boys. Jemmy swung the birdcage, knocking the candle flying. The flame sputtered out in the murky water, and the sewer was thrown into sudden darkness.

"Run for it!" Jemmy yelled out.

"I got one!" cackled Cutwater.

"That's me you got!" bellowed the rat-catcher. "Scurvy riffraff! Who are you?"

Jemmy flattened himself against the wall, and found the prince already there. He heard a splash and a curse as Hold-Your-Nose Billy must have tumbled over Cutwater and the rat-catcher.

In an urgent whisper, the prince asked, "Which way?"

Jemmy made an instant decision. The villains might be able to run them down in this smaller side channel. Back to the main sewer!

He gave the prince's sleeve a quick tug, and the prince reached out for Jemmy's hand.

Off they went, linked together, while the outlaws untangled themselves.

"Which way did they go?" cried out Cutwater.

"Listen for 'em!"

Jemmy froze. He didn't breathe. He waited. And he became suddenly aware of the prince's hand clasped in his own. His first impulse was to withdraw his fingers, but the prince was hanging on for dear life. It was the same as a handshake, and he remembered the prince's own words. It felt friendly and trusting. But, gaw! The wonder of it. Shaking hands with Prince Brat.

"Stop where you stand!" warned Hold-Your-Nose Billy.

"Wherever you are, we'll catch you!" added Cutwater. "You'll never make it out!"

"Which way is out?" snapped the big outlaw.

"The same way you came in," answered the ratcatcher. "Put your back to the breeze from the main sewer."

That was wrong! Good Ol' Tosher, Jemmy thought. He meant to send them off in the opposite direction.

Jemmy tugged on the prince's hand, and they scuttled along the wall toward freedom. A moment later, Jemmy could feel a stronger breeze, and he knew that they were in the main sewer again.

Noses to the breeze, they could make a run for the river. But in his sudden elation, Jemmy banged into the wall with the birdcage.

His hair rose. The clatter was loud enough to wake the dead. Or bring the villains running.

Jemmy made an abrupt turn, pulling the prince deeper into the main sewer. And he whispered, "They'll see us against daylight before we can get out. More holes than wormwood down here. We'll duck into another side tunnel. But if we break loose, don't lose your bearings. The brewery's dead ahead."

The sound of feet sloshing through the water silenced them. Jemmy felt desperately for the mouth of a side tunnel. But Hold-Your-Nose Billy and Cutwater had already rushed out into the main sewer.

"Which way, Billy?" muttered Cutwater.

Jemmy flattened himself against the grave-cold wall, but the prince seemed suddenly to rebel at being chased down like a sewer rat. He yanked the birdcage out of Jemmy's hand and flung it with all his might.

It banged and clattered off the bricks.

In the direction of the brewery.

"What's that?" cried out Cutwater.

"Them is what! Put your back to the breeze. Straight on!"

They barged ahead. Only moments later Ol' Tosher appeared across the great sewer, a fresh candle lit on the bill of his cap.

And then Hold-Your-Nose Billy and Cutwater came flying back.

"I'm bit! I'm bit!"

"Help!"

Grain-fed rats were swarming over the two of them, nipping and biting and clinging like leeches. In the light of the candle, Cutwater waved his arms wildly. He screeched and the hairy outlaw bellowed.

"I declare," said the prince. "They look like they're wearing fur coats."

CHAPTER 20

In which the sun shines and we learn what befell the whipping boy, the prince, and everyone else

Standing in the clear sunshine, the prince breathed in the sweet, fresh air. Then he looked Jemmy squarely in the eyes. "We're going back to the castle."

"Not me! Your pa's put a price on this head o' mine. No, thank you, Prince! I don't fancy doing a jig from the end of a rope."

"Where will you hide for the rest of your life? In the sewers? I'd have them searched, end to end."

Gaw, what a fool he'd been to let the prince in on his best hiding place! Jemmy was on the verge of running—but where to? How far would he get?

"You said you trusted me," declared the prince. "But I can see you didn't mean it."

"I meant it—up to a point."

"Then follow me." It was a command.

Jemmy swallowed hard, and followed. They weren't at the castle gates yet. He'd think of something!

The prince led him back onto the fairgrounds and searched out Betsy and the hot-potato man.

"You've served your prince nobly," he announced.

"What are you talking about, lad?" replied Captain Nips. "Hot-hot-hot potatoes!"

"The king has offered a reward for the whipping boy. Here he stands. Turn him in."

And Jemmy stood dumfounded. He felt betrayed. "Gaw!"

Betsy flashed her eyes. "Turn Jemmy in? I'll do no such thing."

"I command it!"

"Who are you to command anything!"

"I'm—I'm Prince Brat."

"Ha!"

Run for it, Jemmy thought.

Deeply wounded, he gave the prince a last, blazing look. The prince returned a quick, playful wink. It befuddled Jemmy for an instant. And then, in a flash, Jemmy saw that for the first time the prince was up to a kindly piece of mischief.

"Head to toe, he's Prince Brat," said Jemmy. "Better do what he says or he'll have you boiled in oil."

Jemmy had to wait with Betsy, Petunia, and Captain Nips while the prince was alone with the king.

Finally, a pair of golden doors were opened and the group was ushered into the throne room.

The king sat with his legs crossed and the merest flicker of a smile on his lips.

Betsy bowed low, and Captain Nips did the best he could.

"The reward is yours," the king announced, and then he turned to the prince. "What about the bear? Came to your rescue, did he?"

"Couldn't we give him the title of Official Dancing Bear to Your Royal Majesty, Papa? He'd draw crowds wherever he went."

"Done."

Betsy and Captain Nips were dismissed.

Jemmy now stood alone—it seemed hours—while the king gazed at him. He began to feel a noose tightening around his neck.

"You ought to be whipped."

"Yes, My Lord."

"Prince Horace has caused enough mischief to wear out the hides of a dozen whipping boys. He tells me it's thanks to you that he's back, sound and safe. The king thanks you."

Jemmy took a small breath.

"You are placed under the prince's protection under one condition. He has sworn to do his lessons, blow out his night candle, and otherwise behave himself."

Jemmy's eyes flicked to the prince. Gaw! he thought. You must want me for a friend awful bad to promise all that. So help me, if it's a friend you ran off looking for, it's a friend you found!

"Dismissed, both of you," said the king. "But do change out of those smelly clothes."

Retreating toward the golden doors, the prince beside him, Jemmy felt a sparkle rise into his eyes. "You got me off without so much as a single whack," he whispered.

"I couldn't bear all the yowling and bellowing."

"I wouldn't yowl and bellow."

"But *I* would, Jemmy!" And Jemmy caught the twinkle in his eyes.

Almost at the doors, they were stopped by the king's voice. "One more thing!" The king broke into a smile you could warm your hands over. "If you boys decide to run away again, take me with you."

In the days that followed, ballad sellers began to cry out new and final verses to the notorious life of Hold-Your-Nose Billy and his partner, Cutwater.

An old rat-catcher had seen them flee from the sewer. And he'd seen them stow away aboard a ship raising its sails for a long voyage. It was a convict ship bound for a speck of an island in distant waters. A convict island.

 *Note*

Readers often write to ask if a story is true. This tale is a work of the imagination, but the most surprising part of it is true.

Some royal households of past centuries did *keep whipping boys to suffer the punishments due a misbehaving prince. History is alive with lunacies and injustices.*

As Jemmy would say, "Gaw!"